The Very Little Girl

by Phyllis Krasilovsky
pictures by Karen Gundersheimer

Cartwheel
·B·O·O·K·S·™

SCHOLASTIC INC.
New York Toronto London Auckland Sydney

For Alexis, my first very little girl, with love.
P.K.

Text copyright © 1953, renewed 1981, 1992 by Phyllis Krasilovsky.
Illustrations © 1992 by Karen Gundersheimer.
All rights reserved. Published by Scholastic Inc.
CARTWHEEL BOOKS is a trademark of Scholastic Inc.

No part of this publication may be reproduced in whole or in part, or stored in a retrieval system, or transmitted in any form or by any means, electronic, mechanical, photocopying, recording, or otherwise, without written permission of the publisher. For information regarding permission, write to Scholastic Inc., 730 Broadway, New York, NY 10003.

LIBRARY OF CONGRESS CATALOGING-IN-PUBLICATION DATA.
Krasilovsky, Phyllis.
    The very little girl / by Phyllis Krasilovsky ; pictures by Karen Gundersheimer.
        p.   cm.
    Summary: A very little girl gradually grows bigger—big enough to be a big sister to her new baby brother.
    ISBN 0-590-44761-0
    [1. Growth—Fiction.   2. Brothers and sisters—Fiction.]
I. Gundersheimer, Karen, ill.   II. Title.
PZ7.K865Ve   1992
[E]—dc20   91-44949
                                                                      CIP
                                                                       AC

12 11 10 9 8 7 6 5 4 3 2 1   2 3 4 5 6 7/9
Printed in Singapore
First Scholastic printing, September 1992

Once there was a little girl who was very
                                    very
                                       very little.

She was smaller
than a rosebush.

She was smaller than the garden fence.

She was smaller than her wagon.

She was smaller than her mother's desk

and smaller than a rake.

She was too little to ride
on the merry-go-round.

She couldn't feed the lamb at the petting zoo.

She couldn't swing on her swing

or reach the cookie jar in the kitchen.

She had to have a special little chair to sit on and a special little table to eat at

and a special little bed to sleep in.

She was smaller than all the
other little girls on her street.

BUT

One day she could swing!

She could carry a
big bag of groceries.

She was bigger than her dog!

And bigger than her wagon!

Every day after that she found more things which were smaller than she.

The very little girl began to grow BIGGER!

She grew BIGGER than the rosebush.

She could climb over
the garden fence.

She could even rake the leaves by herself.

She was big enough to
ride on the merry-go-round

and feed the lamb at the petting zoo.

She could see the top of her mother's desk.

She could get a cookie all by herself!

She grew too BIG for her special little
chair and her special little table
and her special little bed.

Now she ate at the big table with her
mother and father

and she had a new big bed.

She was no longer a very little girl.

She was big enough to play with the other little girls on her street.

Now she was big enough to be a big
sister to her brand-new baby brother

who was very
       very
          very little!